Withdrawn

TOP 10 TIPS FOR SAFE AND RESPONSIBLE DIGITAL COMMUNICATION

TAMRA B. ORR

ROSEN
PUBLISHING®

NEW YORK

Published in 2013 by The Rosen Publishing Group, Inc.
29 East 21st Street, New York, NY 10010

Copyright © 2013 by The Rosen Publishing Group, Inc.

First Edition

Library of Congress Cataloging-in-Publication Data

Orr, Tamra B.
Top 10 tips for safe and responsible digital communication/Tamra B. Orr.—1st ed.
    p. cm.—(Tips for success)
Includes bibliographical references and index.
ISBN 978-1-4488-6865-0 (lib. bdg.)
1. Internet–Safety measures. 2. Internet–Social aspects. 3. Online etiquette. I. Title.
II. Title: Top ten tips for safe and responsible digital communication.
TK5105.875.I57O77 2013
384.3'30289—dc23

                                                                                2012001101

Manufactured in the United States of America

CPSIA Compliance Information: Batch #S12YA: For further information, contact Rosen Publishing, New York, New York, at
1-800-237-9932.

CONTENTS

INTRODUCTION

A study from the Kaiser Family Foundation found that the average eight- to eighteen-year-old spends seven hours and thirty-eight minutes a day with some kind of media, whether it is the television, the computer, or video games. Victoria Rideout, vice president and director of the Program for the Study of Media and Health at the Kaiser Family Foundation, states, "The thing that jumps out is the enormous amount of time kids spend consuming media. It's more than seven and a half hours a day, seven days a week. That's more than fifty-three hours a week—more time than grown-ups spend in a full-time job."

There is no question that being online is a part of your life. You may be reading content on one Web page while you simultaneously chat, e-mail, and research. You juggle the pages and windows and multitask effortlessly. As Lee Rainie, director of

One of the best ways to keep in touch with family and friends is through video chatting. Not only can you talk with people in real time, but you can also see them as if in face-to-face conversation.

Pew Internet and American Life Research, says, "The media permeates all they [teenagers] do, except when they're sleeping. Theirs is a multimedia life."

The Internet has changed everything, including the way teenagers live their lives, shop, listen to music, watch television and movies, study, research, learn, communicate, and social-ize. The world is now literally at your fingertips, from digging up facts for a class assignment and playing video games with people on the other side of the planet to chatting with a dozen different friends at once and recording a video of your latest song to share with the world. The Internet has unlocked the door to the planet for most people—and there are so many benefits, it is almost impossible to list them all. As soon as you are done, you either think of something else, or someone invents another software app or program to add to the list.

But guess what? There are some downsides to the Internet, too. All of that amazing access comes with a price. You may get to know more people—but not all of them are nice. You may get to see more places, buy more items, or play more games—but they are not always the best choices. The Internet is exciting and educational, but just as in the real world, the virtual world can also be dangerous. Staying safe when exploring the Web is a matter of taking precautions, following some basic rules of safety and etiquette, and speaking up when others don't do the same.

When you get ready to ride your bike to a friend's house, you put on a helmet. When you get in the car to go to the store, you fasten your seatbelt. These are easy ways to stay safe as you explore and participate in the world around you. The same idea applies when you go online. Prepare to have some fun adventures and discover something new and exciting—but do it safely.

KEEP PERSONAL INFORMATION PERSONAL

You've seen them a million times. The familiar boxes pop up on the screen, with drop-down menus to make it extra simple. Just fill in all of those blanks, including your name, address, telephone number, e-mail address, and password. Perhaps they also ask for your birth date, your dog's name, the city you were born in, and other private, personal, and identifying information. How much information is too much? That's a good question and one that even the experts aren't sure how to answer.

TREAD CAUTIOUSLY

When a Web site asks you for personal information, first check that it also requires parental permission if you're under eighteen

WHAT ABOUT PHOTOGRAPHS?

Have you ever posted a photograph of yourself online? Chances are you have, and that's fine. But whenever you do, make sure it is a photo that you won't care if your grandmother sees, or a college recruiter, or a potential employer. If you're doing something you shouldn't be, or behaving in a way that is going to make you blush later, you might not want to put it out there for the whole world to see, possibly forever. Don't post a picture with other people in it without asking their permission first. Remember, if you post images of other people without their permission, they can do the same to you, and then you're bound to end up blushing.

years old. If it doesn't, it is in violation of the Children's Online Privacy Protection Act (COPPA), which has been in effect in the United States since spring 2000. This law originated with the Federal Trade Commission and was designed to regulate companies that had online sites that collected personal information from or about children. The law states that these companies are not allowed to ask for any personal information until the young person is given parental consent.

When you are on a particular Web site and have been asked to provide personal information, first look for the company's privacy policy. Read it and then show it to your parents. Never provide any personal information to a site without discussing it with your parents. They might have certain rules they want you to follow or a list of what is OK and not OK to share.

Remember that when you post information online, it is very hard to know exactly who sees it. Can this information be read by someone

THE VERY WORST PASSWORDS

What passwords rank as the weakest and most vulnerable to hacking? Some of the worst include 1234, 123abc (combining letters and numbers is a good idea, but not in such an obvious sequence), qwerty (the first six letters in the upper left of the keyboard), master, letmein ("let me in"), trustno1 ("trust no one"), and ncc1701 (the number of the Starship Enterprise in *Star Trek*). What is the number one worst password people use when online? You guessed it: password. As Eric Griffith says in his article for *PCMag*, "For the love of all that's techie, if you use 'password' as your password, just sign off the Internet right now."

other than whom you intended? Yes. Can it be traced back to your computer? Yes. Does this mean you can never put personal information on the Web? No. But it does mean you have to do it very carefully and only when you are sure the site you are dealing with is reputable.

GOING BEYOND "20 QUESTIONS"

One of the many reasons it can be dangerous to put too much personal information on the Web is that it can give people too many clues about what your passwords might be. Think about the top twenty questions that a person might ask about you, such as your birthday, pet's name, or best friend's name. There are the "favorite" questions, too, such as your favorite color, book, movie, television show, college, car, or band. All of this information is often what individuals use to create their passwords. So posting that information as part of your Facebook profile or sharing it in a chat room can make it far easier for the cyber "bad

Passwords are supposed to give you protection. It is essential that you choose one that is very difficult to guess or figure out. There are thousands of hackers at work trying to crack your password, so make it a strong one.

guys" to figure out your password and use it for their nasty, even illegal, purposes.

When creating a password, take your time and come up with a few really strong, infallible ones. Passwords are a part of almost everything you do on the Internet, from getting your e-mail and posting to your blog to registering on your favorite sites and logging in to social networking accounts. Remember that the strongest passwords are ones that:

- Use a combination of upper and lowercase letters and numbers
- Are at least eight characters long

- Don't contain your first or last name
- Don't contain a complete word
- Include symbols found on the keyboard and/or spaces
- Change from one site to the next, so one password does not access all of your online accounts

Creating a strong password will help protect your personal information. Not putting that information online in the first place will protect it even more. As the experts remind you, always think before you click.

THINK BEFORE YOU CLICK: DOWNLOADING SAFELY AND LEGALLY

ownloading is quick, easy, and often free—so there has to be a catch somewhere, right? There is. Downloading is like opening your front door when you hear a friendly knock. Sure, chances are that when you open it, your buddies or a trusted neighbor will be standing there. But when you swing that door open to let someone in, a few others might sneak in, too.

AVOIDING MALWARE

Some of these visitors are known as malware—computer viruses and worms. These tricky visitors can damage your furniture, eat up all of your food, and even set your house on fire. In other words, they can damage your files, steal all of your stored information, or even cause your computer's hard drive to melt down. Others who might barge their way through the door uninvited could even be criminals. They are there illegally, and if you allow them entry, even unknowingly and unintentionally, they could get you in trouble with the law. So how do you find out just who is standing on the other side of the door before you open it? Use some common sense and follow the following guidelines.

1. If you didn't ask for it, don't download it.
If a pizza delivery guy is standing out there saying he has three large pepperoni pizzas for you—and you didn't order any—don't open the door. When you're online, all of those unasked-for invitations to download "risk-free" programs are like those pizzas. You didn't ask for them, and most likely they will arrive full of spam, attachments, and lots of other toppings you don't want but will have to pay a very high price for anyway.

2. If you don't know and trust the company, Web site, or source, don't download it.

If your best friend is at the door, sure you can open it. But what if it is your best friend's neighbor's son-in-law's mechanic? Keep the door shut. If you don't know the company or the source of a download, just don't take the risk. Stick with well-known companies. If you aren't sure, there are watchdog Web sites to help you, such as McAfee's Site Advisor (http://www.siteadvisor.com). This free download acts like a bouncer who stands at your front door, determining if your visitors are trustworthy or not. It sits inside your computer and gives you warnings when you attempt to download a possibly harmful program from a dubious site.

3. If you want to download a program, do a background check first.

Someone at the front door wants to hang out with you—nice, but check up on the person first. Go online and either Google the name of the program you want to download or go to the program's Web site. Read the description and recommendations to make sure the program is legitimate and no one has any serious complaints about it. Take a minute and read user forums to find comments about the program. Is everyone telling you that this is the best new program since the invention of slushies—or warning you to run NOW?

LEGAL TUNES

Want to listen to new music but don't have the money to pay for iTunes and other fee-based music download programs? Don't fall into the trap of illegal downloading—it is just WRONG. It is theft. It is stealing. Go to legitimate, legal, and free or very low cost music sites like Pandora, Rhapsody, or streaming Internet radio.

4. If you are going to download something, first back up all of your documents and your system.

Just in case you make the wrong decision and that new visitor ends up trashing your house, make sure you have a backup waiting to help clean up the mess. Save the entire contents of your computer's hard drive to an external hard drive, a flash drive or memory stick, or the cloud. If a virus-bearing download wipes out your computer's hard drive, you will be able to restore it with the backup.

WHAT, ME? A CRIMINAL?!

Simply put, it is not legal to download copyrighted games, music, movies, television shows, or software that you have not paid for and that are privately owned property and not in the public domain. If you got it for free, watch out. If you then share it with your best buds, watch out even more because you may be committing a crime that carries a hefty penalty. Illegal downloading can be

Jammie Thomas-Rasset found out the hard way about the cost of illegal downloading. She shared the blame with her children and ex-boyfriend, all of whom stole about 1,700 songs.

punishable by up to five years in prison and/or $250,000 in fines. Just ask Jammie Thomas-Rasset. She illegally down-loaded twenty-four songs for $1 each. In June 2009, the court fined her $80,000 for each song. Her total fine?—$1.9 million.

One of the biggest perks to the Internet is the ability to grab a song, stream a movie, or add a program to your computer with just a turn of that doorknob—or a click of the mouse. Do it safely, do it legally, and use your common sense. Don't invite just anyone through that virtual front door, or you may find yourself in a very real world of trouble.

BUYER BEWARE: SHOPPING SAFELY AND CAREFULLY

The idea of being able to buy almost anything you want by just pointing and clicking would have seemed like science fiction just a couple of decades ago. Now, it takes just about four or five clicks of a mouse to buy anything imaginable, from books and music to weekly groceries and a brand-new car. Not only is it easy, but you can do it whenever you want because the Internet is open for business twenty-four hours a day, seven days a week. The selection is mind-boggling, and shipping is fast (and sometimes free!).

RULES TO LIVE—AND SHOP—BY

Remember, however, that buying online usually means taking a risk because you usually have to provide lots of personal information to pay for and complete a purchase and arrange for shipping. This information includes where you live, your phone number, e-mail address, and credit card information. How can you shop online, without giving the wrong people your personal identifying and financial information? Here are some of the most important rules to remember:

1. Do NOT order anything using your parents' credit cards without checking with them first.
If you haven't checked in with your parents first about using their money, you are in imminent danger of an apocalyptic parental freak-out. So please—ask and get a yes first.

2. Only order from familiar, trusted Web sites.
Remember those strangers standing on your front steps, knocking on the door and asking to be let in? When you purchase items online, they are pounding on the door and yelling, "PAY ME!" In that case, you really, REALLY want to make sure these are people you trust.

3. Make sure the site you are ordering from has a secure sockets layer (SSL) encryption.

2/1/2010 18:02
payments.ebay.com uses VeriSign services as follows:

SITE NAME:	payments.ebay.com
SSL CERTIFICATE STATUS:	Valid (26-Aug-2009 to 26-Aug-2011)
COMPANY/ ORGANIZATION:	EBAY INC. San Jose California, US

Encrypted Data Transmission
This Web site can secure your private information using a VeriSign SSL Certificate. Information exchanged with any address beginning with https is encrypted using SSL before transmission.

Identity Verified
EBAY INC. has been verified as the owner or operator of the Web site located at payments.ebay.com. Official records confirm EBAY INC. as a valid business.

That checkmark in the upper lefthand corner of this Web site (www.verisign.com) is not just another graphic. It is a certified guarantee that the site is honest, reliable, and well-protected.

It sounds like something you would buy at the hardware store, but an SSL encryption is a sign that a site is relatively secure. The site's address will read https:// (not just http://), and an icon of a locked padlock will appear either next to the address or in the status bar at the bottom of the browser. This indicates that the site has the proper protection to make ordering from it a safe process.

4. Only provide the necessary information to purchase your item.

The Web site will need your name, address, and credit card information. However, it does not need to know your birthday, your mother's maiden name, or your Social Security number. Don't give any site more information than it needs to process and complete a purchase.

CREATING AN INTERNET SAFETY PLEDGE

In an attempt to help young people stay safe on the Net, a number of different organizations have set up safety pledges, including the Girl Scouts, the National Crime Prevention Council, and Working to Halt Online Abuse/Kids-Teen Division. You can use any of these or create your own, like the one below.

(1) I will **THINK** before I post and will not post any information or images that might put me at risk, embarrass me, or damage my reputation now or in the future.

(2) I will **RESPECT** other people with whom I interact online. This includes not posting anything rude, threatening, embarrassing, or personal. At the same time, I will **PROTECT** myself online, and if anyone does anything threatening, offensive, or embarrassing to me, I will report it to a trusted adult immediately.

(3) I will be **CAREFUL** about the idea of meeting online friends face-to-face. I will tell a trusted adult about it, and if I decide to meet an online friend, I will arrange to do so in a very public place and have an adult go with me.

_____   _____
Signature   Today's Date

5. Watch out for the scammers—they are definitely out there.

A good rule of thumb: if it sounds too good to be true, be completely assured that it is. Scammers are clever. They will create Web sites that are spelled almost like the one you are looking for (e.g., BestBuy.com becomes BestBy.com) or add a different ending (BestBuy.com becomes BestBuy.net).

6. Read the small print.

Take the time to carefully read the fine print on the Web sites from which you order. Check out their privacy statements (Do they sell your info to other companies?), return policies (Is it hard? Is there a "re-stocking" fee?), and their terms of agreement. Finally, if you have a problem, report it. You can do this through the Federal Trade Commission's hotline (800-382-4357) or Web site (http://www.ftc.gov), or file a report with the Internet Crime Complaint Center (http://www.ic3.gov).

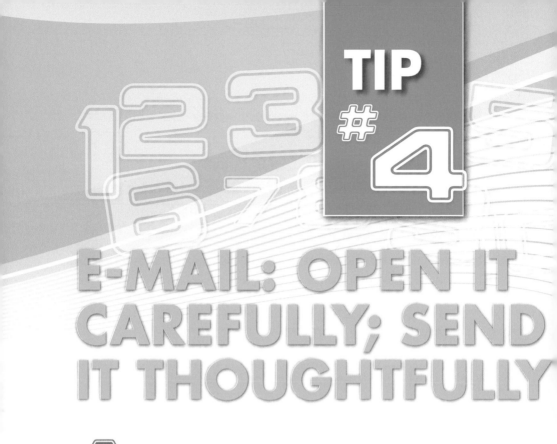

E-MAIL: OPEN IT CAREFULLY; SEND IT THOUGHTFULLY

At one time, getting a message sent from one side of the country to the other took months—if it made it there at all. Mail traveled by horse and had to get through obstacles like blinding blizzards, raging rivers, and towering mountain peaks. Over time, thanks to the development of trains, automobiles, and airplanes, the U.S. Postal Service was able to deliver messages from one place to another in just two to three days—or even overnight.

Impressive as this is, however, all of it pales in comparison to e-mail. E-mail doesn't take days—or even hours. Often it doesn't even take a single minute. A person in another country can send a message and have it appear halfway around the world in mere seconds. Amazing? Absolutely. Completely safe? Nope. There are two main problems with e-mail: spamming and phishing.

TEACHING ONLINE SAFETY: MIXED RESULTS

In 2011, a group called the National Cyber Security Alliance conducted a survey to see how well the nation's schools were teaching students about the importance of online safety. More than one thousand teachers and four hundred principals and superintendents responded. The survey results revealed some disagreement between teachers and administrators. For example, 81 percent of administrators felt like their schools were doing a decent job of instructing students in online safety, but only 51 percent of teachers agreed. Far more principals and superintendents (85 percent) thought online safety should be taught in the classroom than did teachers (55 percent).

"Adding one more thing [to the school day] is always a challenge, [so] I think it clearly has to be embedded in the way we do our teaching and learning," said Keith Kruger, head of the Consortium for School Networking. "As a country, in the school and at the classroom level, we need to be much better at really preparing kids to live in an unfiltered world."

BLOCKING SPAM

Spam is a lot like the commercials that keep interrupting your favorite TV shows. They are distracting and annoying messages sent to your e-mail account that are trying to sell you something you probably don't want or need. The number of spam messages sent out every year is astounding. According to Spam Laws (http://www.spamlaws.com), 14.5 billion spam messages are sent globally every single day. Almost half of all the e-mail sent out daily is spam. Here are some simple ways to reduce the amount of spam sent to your e-mail account:

- Use a spam filter or spam blocker.
- Never, ever reply to or click on the links in a spam message.
- Only click the potentially deceptive "unsubscribe" link if it mentions the CAN-SPAM Act.
- Preview your message, and if you see spam, hit the delete key.

LET'S NOT GO PHISHING

Phishing is one of the fastest-growing crimes on the Internet. In 2007, there were fifty-nine million phishing e-mails sent out every day, netting criminals billions of dollars. A phishing scam is one that arrives in a message that looks like it came from someplace familiar, like your bank, school, social network,

Spam is what often gives e-mail a bad name. These annoying—and sometimes dangerous and criminally fraudulent—messages will fill up your Inbox and you have to spend time hitting the delete key over and over.

e-mail provider, a government agency, a favorite online retailer, or other trusted source. Statistics show that 95 percent of phishing e-mails will look like they are from Amazon, eBay, or banks.

This scam will try to get important personal and financial information from you in the hopes of emptying your bank accounts, using your credit cards, sending e-mails to all of your friends under your name, or committing other types of identity theft and fraud. Another variation on phishing is known as vishing and involves similar requests for personal identifying and financial information over a landline telephone from someone impersonating a representative of your bank, credit card company, favorite charity, or other trusted institution.

How can you prevent falling for these scams? Here are some simple steps:

- Legitimate sources will not ask you to send sensitive information via e-mail. If they ask you to, report the incident to a higher authority, like local law enforcement, the Federal Communications Commission (FCC), Federal Bureau of Investigation (FBI), or Better Business Bureau (BBB).
- Legitimate sources claiming to be your bank or credit card company will not direct you to another Web site or phone number that does not match the ones you have listed on your bank or credit statements or those you have used before when communicating with the company.

- Watch for mistakes in grammar, spelling, and punc-tuation. Legitimate companies rigorously edit their mailings, and mistakes are rare. Phony and fraudulent e-mails are often riddled with odd mistakes and errors.
- The words "Urgent" or "Secret," or "Act Now" are major red flags, especially if accompanied by lots of exclamation points.

When in doubt, go to the actual, legitimate Web site of the organization that claims to be e-mailing you and check in with it. You can also call the organization's customer service line. Ninety-nine percent of the time, organizations will tell you that no, that e-mail is NOT theirs and they have received reports of similar fraudulent e-mail activity. Delete the phony e-mail immediately, and then delete it from your Deleted box. Do not respond to it, even if it is to say that you're onto them.

THE OTHER SIDE OF E-MAIL: SENDING

You know good manners are important whenever your grandpar-ents come over for dinner or you're talking to a college admissions officer on the phone. Those manners, called "etiquette," are also important when you are online, where they are known as "netiquette."

Just as you have to be responsible for what e-mails you open up, you have the same responsibility not to send or for-ward e-mails that can cause other people trouble. Don't send an attachment without contacting people to explain what it is and why you're sending it. Don't forward photos, videos, links, and other information without doing the same. Receiving e-mail attachments from friends and relatives lull the receiver into opening whatever comes into his or her e-mail in-box without exercising caution. This is a bad habit that can come back to haunt the user if he or she accidentally downloads a virus when opening an attachment. However, even some of the seemingly harmless jokes, photos, or videos you forward may be offensive to the person to whom you are sending them.

Some other basic rules of netiquette include:

- Spell-check and proofread your messages.
- DON'T WRITE IN ALL CAPS BECAUSE IT SOUNDS LIKE YOU ARE SHOUTING.
- Do not flame (personally insult) anyone or respond to those who do.

THINK BEFORE YOU SPEAK: CHATTING SAFELY AND RESPONSIBLY

alking to your friends has never been easier. If you aren't texting or calling them on your cell or sending off a quick e-mail, you can connect through instant messaging or social networking chat programs. You can talk about anything—and with your friends, that's fine. But what happens when you don't really know the person on the other end of the conversation?

Sure, you think you do. You've been chatting for months, right? You know his favorite song, what toppings he likes on his pizza, why he gets into arguments with his brother, and what colleges he has applied to so far. He knows your SAT scores, who you've had a crush on for the last two months, and why you have read the Lord of the Rings trilogy four times. You've shared tons of information. So you're friends, right? Well, no, not quite.

One of the coolest things about the Internet is that it makes it possible to talk to people all over the world, instantaneously and in real time. Unfortunately, it also makes it quite possible for those people to lie to you about who they are. They may be a different gender and age than what they have told you. They may live closer or farther away. They may genuinely want to be friends with you because you run wicked raids together in the same *World of Warcraft* guild, or they may be a sexual predator looking for the next victim. It happens all the time, unfortunately. In fact, a study published in the *Journal of the American Medical Association* states, "Nearly one in five American youths who surfed the Net regularly were the targets of unwanted sexual attention."

STAYING SAFE IN A SCARY CYBERWORLD

How do you know whom you're actually talking to when you are chatting online? The honest truth is, most of the time you can't be sure, so you have to really protect yourself. Online predators aren't just dangerous—they are also often quite clever. They befriend young people by being charming. They understand what you're going through. They like the same music you do. They listen to you when others won't and offer decent advice, slowly building rapport and friendship. Too often, this ends in absolute disaster. So, how do you protect yourself?

Social networking sites are hugely popular and a wonderful way to keep in close contact with friends. However, they also open the door to communicating with many people who may not be trustworthy.

- Use a screen name, rather than your real one.
- Don't share information about where you live or what school you attend.
- Don't exchange photos.
- Never share your password.
- Never agree to meet a person face-to-face.
- Tell your parents right away if the person says anything frightening, threatening, or just "weird."
- Never accept flaming of yourself or of others.
- Only respond to private messages in a chat room with extreme caution.
- Know how to block or ignore a person in a chat room.

A NEW KIND OF BULLY

Another complication of being able to talk to so many people online is the risk of cyberbullying. Being cyberbullied is being threatened or intimidated by another computer user. It can be done directly—a message sent directly from one person to another—or by proxy, when the bully encourages others to initiate an attack or gang up on the person.

CYBERBULLYING STATS

- More than one in three young people has experienced cyber-threats online.
- Only one in ten teens tells his or her parents about being cyberbullied.
- The most common type of cyberbullying is making mean comments and spreading rumors.
- About half of young people have experienced some form of cyberbullying, and 10 to 20 percent experience it regularly.

Any kind of bullying—Internet-based or face-to-face—is wrong, and the consequences can be extremely serious. Bullies can be expelled or arrested, their future college and employment prospects destroyed. And the victims of bullying can be psychologically scarred, their grades can suffer, and they may even harm themselves. Some bullying victims have felt so tormented that they committed suicide.

The Stop Cyberbullying organization teaches students to "Take 5!" when they are feeling upset online. It reminds computer users who have been annoyed, angered, or upset to "Drop the mouse, step away from the computer, and no one will get hurt!" This is good advice. If you're ever threatened, speak up! Tell a trusted adult (a teacher, guidance counselor, parent), notify the administrator of the Web site or the Internet service provider, and avoid all communication with the people who are bullying you. If you've been flaming someone and are feeling aggressive and angry, get up, walk away, take some deep breaths, and calm down. Then apologize and never indulge this behavior again.

CONTROL THE CAMERA: USING SKYPE AND VIDEO CHATTING SAFELY AND RESPONSIBLY

nline chatting used to be done with messy bed hair, no makeup, and your holey *Star Trek* PJs that you outgrew two years ago. Not anymore. Thanks to the combination of Web cameras and programs like Skype or Windows Live Messenger, the people you are talking to can now hear you and see you in all your glory.

NATIONAL CYBER SECURITY AWARENESS MONTH

Each October since 2004, the National Cyber Security Alliance has sponsored Cybersecurity Awareness Month (http://www.staysafeonline.org/ncsam). A variety of events are held throughout the country to raise awareness about Internet dangers and how to stay safe in cyberspace. The organization holds classes for individuals and businesses and provides free fact sheets.

ARE YOU READY FOR YOUR CLOSE-UP?

In some ways, having video added to your chatting has helped solve a few problems. For example, if the person claiming to be a sixteen-year-old girl with the cute freckles and long, blonde hair is really a forty-four-year-old guy with prison tattoos and greasy hair, you will certainly find out immediately. Also, when people are watching each other on camera, they are typically less likely to get hostile or act offensively and are more likely to use good netiquette.

Of course, having a camera right in front of you may bring out your inner rock star, too. You may find yourself singing a new song for friends, showing them some new dance moves, or engaging in a wild air guitar solo. That's fine—but you have to know where to draw the line. Video cams are also a tempting invitation to show much more than the new jumps you just

Being able to see who you are talking to can be exciting and fun—but it can also inspire some people to reveal far more than they should. Don't do anything in front of the camera that you wouldn't want your teachers, parents, or grandparents to see.

learned at parkour class. They can inspire some young people to reveal skin and personal body parts that they shouldn't, and that can lead to trouble for everyone involved.

Just as you don't want to open up an e-mail from an unknown sender in your in-box, you don't want to accept a video chat invitation from someone you don't know. Video chatting programs often feature privacy settings that allow you to say who and who cannot contact you. Go to Preferences and limit that list to only the people you know and trust.

DON'T OVER-SHARE: BLOGGING AND VLOGGING SAFELY AND RESPONSIBLY

Just as letters have yielded to e-mails and turntables have evolved into MP3 players, diaries and journals have been transformed into blogs and vlogs (video blogs). Blogs and vlogs are where you get to rant and rave about the ups and downs of life, share your enthusiasms, vent your frustrations, and generally express yourself on any and all subjects that interest you.

FUN AND GAMES—WITH A MESSAGE

The National Center for Missing and Exploited Children makes learning about safety on the Net fun at its NS Teens Web site (http://www.nsteens. org). The site features games, videos, comics, and teaching materials. Check it out!

CONSIDER YOUR AUDIENCE

Most blogs and vlogs are read and watched by only a handful of people (usually a close circle of family and friends), but if they are public, others can potentially see them—people like your parents, teachers, or even potential employers. When nineteen-year-old Jenny Rypkema discovered that her parents were reading her blog, she was upset, but her father, Chris Rypkema, told *USA Today*, "You put something out on the Web with expectations that even complete strangers are going to come by and read it. Why be surprised if your parent is going to take an interest in you as an individual and wants to know more about you? Her blog was a way I could keep in touch with her." If you aren't prepared for a wider audience to read what you write or watch your videos, set your blog and vlog to private so that only those who are invited by you can access them.

Diaries used to come with actual locks and keys to help make sure they stayed private and personal. Today, many teens put the same kind of information they once hid away under lock and key out on the Web for all the world to see. Just remember, there is no telling how far your words might travel, how long they will linger and be accessible to anyone who searches your name. There is no way to know how many people will be privy to your most personal reflections, opinions, and confessions.

BE DISCREET

While pouring out your thoughts, dreams, and concerns about life onto your blog and across cyberspace is often quite fun, try to resist the urge to overshare. It is OK to say your father is struggling at work, but if you put the details of his coworkers' arguments online, especially if you add

Sharing with your friends is wonderful. Sharing too much and with too many people is dangerous. Those words you type may reach all the way around the world.

company names, it can cause big problems. It is OK to mention that your family is planning to go on vacation, but listing the days and times and how long you will be gone is not wise. Stay vague.

Also be aware that people are likely to post comments on your blog or vlog in response to what you have written, and not everyone is polite. They may flame you, so be prepared to ignore harsh or critical comments. Don't engage the writer or get drawn into an increasingly nasty war of words.

10 GREAT QUESTIONS
TO ASK A SCHOOLTEACHER

1 WHAT KIND OF PASSWORD SHOULD I USE WHEN SETTING UP AN ONLINE ACCOUNT?

2 HOW DO I KNOW WHAT IS SAFE AND NOT SAFE TO DOWNLOAD?

3 SHOULD I EVER MEET AN ONLINE FRIEND FACE-TO-FACE?

4 WHAT ARE SOME OF THE SIGNS THAT THE PERSON I'M COMMUNICATING WITH IS ACTUALLY AN ONLINE PREDATOR?

5 WHAT PERSONAL INFORMATION IS OK TO SHARE WHEN ONLINE?

6 WHAT SHOULD I DO IF SOMEONE SAYS SOMETHING OFFENSIVE TO ME ONLINE?

7 WHAT IS CYBERBULLYING AND WHAT CAN I DO ABOUT IT?

8 WHAT QUALIFIES AS A BULLYING MESSAGE?

9 HOW AND TO WHOM DO I REPORT THREATENING OR ABUSIVE ONLINE BEHAVIOR?

10 IF I REPORT AN INCIDENT TO A TIP LINE, WHAT HAPPENS NEXT?

TIP #8

OBSERVE PROPER SOCIAL NETWORKING ETIQUETTE AND SAFETY PRECAUTIONS

Long, long ago (just ask your parents), if you wanted to know if someone liked you and wanted to be your friend, you wrote a note, folded it into a tiny square, and secretly passed it to the person during class. The receiver could either check "Yes, I do" or "No, I don't." Today, the same message is sent via social networking sites like Twitter and Facebook, allowing you to "friend" and "unfriend" someone at will. Getting "friended" is a good feeling, but being bumped off someone's list and "unfriended," or just having your polite "friend me" request ignored, isn't such a great feeling.

SOCIAL NETWORKING BY THE NUMBERS

- One out of every six minutes spent online is spent on a social networking site.
- Facebook currently reaches 73 percent of the total U.S. Internet population each month.
- Sixty percent of social media–using teens believe their peers are basically nice to each other on social networking sites, but 88 percent have seen someone be cruel to another person on these same sites. Twelve percent of teens say that they have seen cruelty frequently.
- Thirty-three percent of all Internet-initiated sex crimes involved social networking sites.
- Forty-one percent of social media–using teens have experienced at least one "real world" negative outcome (face-to-face arguments with friends or parents, physical fights, trouble in school) as a result of using a social networking site.

Just as with face-to-face social encounters, online social networking requires good manners and proper etiquette. If, for example, you have decided that you don't want to be "friended" with someone anymore, don't make a big deal out of it. Either just let people stay on the list and ignore their posts or officially "unfriend" them. Don't make flaming comments in the process or post a long explanation. Be a good "netizen" and always show good manners, compassion, and kindness when online.

Wanting to unfriend someone is normal—your relationships are fluid and changing. "Unfriending" may be a difficult and awkward process. But it can also be necessary and, ultimately, healthy, honest, and genuine. Dr. Larry Rosen, author of *Rewired: Understanding the iGeneration and the Way They Learn*, told CNN, "Friends and acquaintances come and go as we move through life stages and find the need for keeping some friends and losing others. If you had no way to unfriend someone, then this would lose the authenticity of having a relationship."

SAFE NETWORKING

Social networking pages are easier to access online than a personal blog. So watch what you say on your wall, especially if you "friend" people indiscriminately, accepting any and all offers of online friendship. You really don't know who chose to look you up today and see what you're up to. It may be your former next-door neighbor who hasn't seen you since you were three and wants to share sentimental memories or a long-lost best friend from grade school who wants to reconnect. Great! But it could also be that creepy guy you met at the gas station who wanted your phone number. If you happen to post your status as "Home alone all afternoon and nothing to do," you could be opening yourself up for trouble. Also, refrain from talking negatively about specific people. What if you complained about your aunt's disappointing birthday present to you, and her son—your cousin—reads it and passes it on to his mother?

What can you do to stay safe online, protecting both your physical self and your friendships and relationships from harm?

- Keep your profile set to "private."
- When someone wants to "friend" you, don't automatically accept. Would you want to spend time with this person face-to-face? If not, just ignore the request.
- Never post personal information like your address, credit card information, or passwords.
- If something feels wrong, don't ignore this gut feeling. Tell a trusted adult immediately.
- Think long and hard before posting information on your status. Is there information there that could harm you if the wrong person read it?
- Don't write anything about anyone else that you wouldn't want to read if someone had written it about you.
- Think carefully before you post anything. If what you've written is emotional or negative in any way, give yourself a couple of hours before posting it. Revisit it after you've calmed down and decide if it's still something you want the world to see.

FACE-TO-FACE?

OK, you know it was bound to happen—someone you met online wants to meet face-to-face. If you absolutely want this to happen and your parents give their permission, please take every precaution before doing so.

- Seek and receive your parents' permission.
- Ask your friends about this person. Do they know him or her?

- Look online for this person. Is there a profile you can read?
- Meet only in a very public place during the daytime hours.
- Take a trusted adult with you or a group of friends. Never, ever go alone.
- Tell someone where you're going, who you're meeting, and when you'll be home.
- Take your cell phone.

THE REAL WORLD

Hanging out with your friends online, checking statuses, posting news, looking up people you've just met online or in person—all

Some of the biggest critics of today's high-tech world worry that computer networking will replace spending time out in the world with friends. Digital communication is fantastic, but it is not the same as hanging out in the real world with the people you like the best.

of these are great. But they cannot beat actually spending time with friends and family together, face-to-face. Don't let clicking on a profile to check on a friend's current status replace the time you would spend riding your bike to his house, meeting at the mall, or going to a movie. Computers and the Internet are wonderful tools for round-the-clock communication and socializing—but they aren't real life. Friendships and family relationships grow, develop, and thrive in the light of day, in face-to-face conversation, and shared experiences and adventures out in the real world.

KEEP IT SHORT AND KNOW YOUR PLACE:
USING MICROBLOGGING AND LOCATION-BASED SERVICES

First you could post text, pictures, links, and short videos to your blog. Then you could pour all this information into your networking site status reports. And now you can use services like Twitter, Foursquare, and Gowalla to post your thoughts, provide status updates, and announce your current precise location.

REPORTING TO THE CYBER TIP LINE

What happens when you combine the Federal Bureau of Investigation, the Department of Homeland Security (DHS), the U.S. Postal Inspection Service (USPIS), the Internet Crimes Against Children (ICAC) Task Force, the U.S. Secret Service, and the U.S. Department of Justice's Child Exploitation and Obscenity Section (CEOS)? You get the Cyber Tip Line, a method for reporting incidents of child sexual exploitation, including child pornography and online enticement. It is available twenty-four hours a day, seven days a week. You can leave a tip by visiting the CyberTipline section of the Web site of the National Center for Missing and Exploited Children.

BREVITY IS THE SOUL OF WIT

These microblogging and location-based services allow you to blog—in brief—about your life, opinions, obsessions, and current location using very few words (Twitter's limit is 140 characters) via your computer, smartphone, or tablet. The character limit forces users to focus on being precise and pithy instead of wordy and long-winded, as in many conventional blogs. Microblogging has certainly caught on—politicians, corporations, stores, and celebrities all use it to keep their fans and customers up-to-date on their activities.

Microblogging carries with it the same risks and precautions that other types of blogging and social networking sites do. Before posting, always think about who is going to read your messages, and don't give out too much information. Don't overshare details about where you are and what you're doing in case there are people reading those updates who may take advantage of the data. Don't agree to meet an online microblogger in person without taking the same precautions listed in the previous chapter. Just because your messages are incredibly short doesn't mean they can't do a huge amount of damage. And try not to get carried away with sending out too many messages, trying the patience of even your most devoted friends and "followers."

Can you relay how you are feeling, what you are doing, where you are, or who you are in 140 characters or less? Microblogging and location-based services allow you to do just that.

MYTHS & FACTS

MYTH: INTERNET PREDATORS ARE USUALLY SO OBVIOUS THAT THEY ARE EASY TO AVOID.

FACT: UNFORTUNATELY, INTERNET PREDATORS ARE NOT NASTY, OBNOXIOUS, THREATENING TYPES ONLINE. INSTEAD, THEY TEND TO BE CHARMING AND FRIENDLY AND SPECIALIZE IN "GROOMING" YOUNG PEOPLE BY MAKING THEM FEEL UNDERSTOOD AND APPRECIATED.

MYTH: THANKS TO LAWS LIKE THE CHILDREN'S ONLINE PRIVACY PROTECTION ACT (COPPA), WEB SITES CREATED FOR CHILDREN ARE ALWAYS CLOSELY MONI-TORED AND COMPLETELY SAFE TO USE.

FACT: WHILE LAWS LIKE COPPA HAVE DONE A GREAT DEAL TO MAKE THE NET A SAFER PLACE, THEY ARE NOT PERFECT. DESPITE THE LAWS IN PLACE, WEB SITES ARE NOT ALWAYS CLOSELY MONITORED AND SAFE.

MYTH: CYBERBULLYING IS JUST A NATURAL PART OF BEING A KID AND DOESN'T ACTUALLY HURT ANYONE.

FACT: BULLYING IS MEAN AND DANGEROUS AND HURTS EVERYONE INVOLVED, WHETHER IT IS DONE FACE-TO-FACE OR OVER THE NET. IT CANNOT BE ALLOWED, AND ANY INCIDENTS SHOULD BE REPORTED SO THAT THE BULLYING CAN BE STOPPED IMMEDIATELY.

CONTROL, FILTER, AND PROTECT:
OPTIMIZING THE USE OF CONTROLS, FILTERS, AND ANTIVIRUS PROGRAMS

Y ou've been responsible. You've taken precautions. You're careful whenever you go on the Net. It's a lot of responsibility to shoulder all by yourself, though, so how about a little help? A number of companies offer a variety of parental controls, monitors, and filters to help safeguard Web browsing and usage.

LOOKING OVER YOUR SHOULDER

According to the 2011 Parent-Teen Internet Safety Study published by GFI Software, 36 percent of parents use some type of monitoring software or filter so that they can watch what their teens do online and block inappropriate sites.

SUBMITTING AN ANONYMOUS TIP ONLINE

What should you do if you or someone you know has (1) been sent any kind of child pornography, (2) been sexually approached by someone who knows you are a minor, or (3) received sexually explicit images from someone who knows you are a minor? Report it! The FBI recommends that you contact your local or state law enforcement agency immediately. You can also notify the FBI directly by visiting its Web site and going to the "Tips and Public Leads" page. Through the FBI, you can also access links that allow you to report cyber scams and incidents of fraud to local field offices.

While this may seem overly intrusive and controlling, some teens are secretly grateful for this. The knowledge of parental oversight reduces temptation, provides motivation for good behavior, and provides a sense of security. Teens know their parents love them and care about them enough to be vigilant and protective. Each family works differently, and how your family deals with the very real threats that exist in cyberspace might not work for your best friend—or even for your brother or sister. That is something you will have to work out with your parents through an ongoing combination of open communication, honesty, understanding, and compromise.

ANTIVIRUS SOFTWARE

A recent nationwide survey revealed that 65 percent of families reported that their home computers had been infected by a virus, and more than half of them said it had happened to them

It is vitally important to have an up-to-date antivirus program installed on your computer. It will help protect your computer—its hard drive; its software; and all the sensitive, personal, and identifying information contained within.

more than once. Many companies offer antivirus software that regularly scans a computer's hard drive for any possible viruses and other malware. Antivirus software can help make sure that malware cannot get into your computer.

Your computer really is a portal to the wider world, both actual and virtual. You open it by clicking the mouse, and suddenly, the entire planet is yours to explore. While friends, family, and fascination are all out there, so are those unwanted visitors, hackers, fraudsters, flamers, bullies, predators, thieves, and criminals. By all means, explore the infinite universe that is cyberspace, and play away! But play it safe. Always.

GLOSSARY

ATTACHMENT A document, photo, or any other piece of information contained within digital files that can be "attached" to an e-mail and sent to other computer users.

COPYRIGHT The legal right to publish works or perform art, and the right to allow others to do so.

CYBERSPACE A worldwide system of computer networks in which online communication takes place. It is frequently used to describe the Internet.

DOWNLOAD To retrieve a program, document, or file from a Web site or e-mail and save it to your computer.

ETIQUETTE The polite way to behave in society.

FLAME To make a harsh online personal attack on someone, often in a blog's comment section or a chat room, that can be viewed by many other people.

INTERNET PREDATOR Someone who uses e-mails, Web sites, video links, or social networking sites to reach people for the purpose of doing harm to them.

LOCATION-BASED SERVICE (LBS) A social network based on sharing one's location with other users in real-time.

MALWARE Software designed to infiltrate, control, ransack, or otherwise damage a computer.

MICROBLOG A social networking program that allows for the posting of very short messages (often 140 characters or less).

NETIQUETTE The manners to use and code of proper behavior to observe when using the Internet.

NETIZEN A person who uses the Internet.

PHISHING The sending of e-mails that are designed to look trustworthy but are in fact an attempt to get the recipient to yield personal identifying and financial information.

SOFTWARE The information and programs used to direct the operation of a computer.

SPAM Unsolicited e-mails designed to sell a product or service.

STREAM To send information (usually an audio or video file) over the Internet in a continuous stream, allowing users to watch video clips, vlogs, TV programs, and films, and listen to songs, podcasts, audio blogs, and radio broadcasts.

TWITTER A popular social networking application in which users broadcast messages of no more than 140 characters to their "followers" (other users who join someone's Twitter feed and receive that person's tweets).

VISHING The sending of false messages over landline telephones designed to encourage recipients to provide personal identifying and financial information.

Family Online Safety Institute (FOSI)
815 Connecticut Avenue, Suite 220
Washington, DC 20006
(202) 572-6252
Web site: http://www.fosi.org
The Family Online Safety Institute is an international
   nonprofit organization that works to develop a
   safer Internet for children and families. It works
   to influence public policies and educate the
   public.

Get Net Wise
Internet Education Foundation
1634 I Street NW
Washington, DC 20009
Web site: http://www.getnetwise.org
Get Net Wise is part of the Internet Education
   Foundation, which works to provide a safe online
   environment for children and families.

International Technology Education Association (ITEA)
1914 Association Drive, Suite 201
Reston, VA 20191-1539
(703) 860-2100
Web site: http://www.iteaconnect.org
The International Technology Education Association
   promotes technology education and literacy.

Internet Education Foundation
1634 I Street NW, Suite 1100
Washington, DC 20006
(202) 637-0968
Web site: http://neted.org
The Internet Education Foundation is a nonprofit
    organization dedicated to informing the public about
    Internet education.

Internet Keep Safe Coalition
1401 K Street NW, Suite 600
Washington, DC 20005
(866) 794-7233
Web site: http://www.ikeepsafe.org
The Internet Keep Safe Coalition is an educational
    resource for children and families that educates
    about Internet safety and ethics associated with
    Internet technologies.

i-SAFE Inc.
5900 Pasteur Court, Suite #100
Carlsbad, CA 92008
(760) 603-7911
Web site: http://www.isafe.org
Founded in 1998, i-SAFE Inc. is the leader in Internet
    safety education. Available in all fifty states,
    Washington, D.C., and Department of Defense

schools across the world, i-SAFE is a nonprofit foundation whose mission is to educate and empower youth to make their Internet experiences safe and responsible. The goal is to educate students on how to avoid dangerous, inappropriate, or unlawful online behavior.

Media Awareness Network
1500 Merivale Road, 3rd Floor
Ottawa, ON K2E 6Z5
Canada
(613) 224-7721
Web site: http://www.media-awareness.ca
The Media Awareness Network creates media literacy programs for young people. Its site contains educational games about the Internet and media.

Public Safety Canada
Attn: Public Safety Portal—SafeCanada.ca
269 Laurier Avenue
West Ottawa, ON K1A 0P8
Canada
(800) 755-7047
Web site: http://www.safecanada.ca
SafeCanada is part of the Canadian government's online efforts to make Canada a safe place for all of its citizens wherever they are—including when they visit cyberspace.

WEB SITES

Due to the changing nature of Internet links, Rosen Publishing has developed an online list of Web sites related to the subject of this book. This site is updated regularly. Please use this link to access the list:

http://www.rosenlinks.com/top10/digcom

Bailey, Diane. *Cyber Ethics*. New York, NY: Rosen Central, 2008.

Cindrich, Sharon, and Ali Douglass. *A Smart Girl's Guide to the Internet: How to Connect with Friends, Find What You Need, and Stay Safe Online* (American Girl Library). Middleton, WI: American Girl Publishing, 2009.

Furgang, Kathy. *Netiquette: A Student's Guide to Digital Etiquette*. New York, NY: Rosen Central, 2011.

Gregson, Susan R. *Cyber Literacy: Evaluating the Reliability of Data*. New York, NY: Rosen Central, 2008.

Hile, Lori. *Social Networks and Blogs* (Mastering Media). Chicago, IL: Heinemann Raintree, 2010.

Hillstrom, Laurie. *Online Social Networks* (Technology 360). Farmington Hills, MI: Lucent/Gale, 2010.

Jacobs, Thomas A. *Teen Cyberbullying Investigated: Where Do Your Rights End and Consequences Begin?* Minneapolis, MN: Free Spirit Publishing, 2010.

Kaplan, Arie. *Blogs: Finding Your Voice, Finding Your Audience*. New York, NY: Rosen Central, 2012.

Kiesbye, Stefan. *Are Social Networking Sites Harmful?* Farmington Hills, MI: Greenhaven Press, 2011.

Roddel, Victoria. *Internet Safety Kids' Guide*. Raleigh, NC: Lulu.com, 2011.

Rogers, Vanessa. *Cyberbullying: Activities to Help Children and Teens to Stay Safe in a Texting,*

Twittering, Social Networking World. London, England: Jessica Kingsley Publishers, 2010.

Ryan, Peter K. *Social Networking* (Digital and Information Literacy). New York, NY: Rosen Central, 2011.

Sandler, Corey. *Living with the Internet and Online Dangers*. New York, NY: Checkmark Books, 2010.

Waters, John K. *The Everything Guide to Social Media: All You Need to Know About Participating in Today's Most Popular Online Communities*. Avon, MA: Adams Media, 2010.

Watkins, Heidi. *Social Networking* (Issues That Concern You). Farmington Hills, MI: Greenhaven Press, 2011.

Wilkinson, Colin. *Twitter and Microblogging: Instant Communication in 140 Characters or Less*. New York, NY: Rosen Central, 2012.

Willard, Nancy. *Cyberbullying and Cyberthreats: Responding to the Challenge of Online Social Aggression, Threats, and Distress*. Champaign, IL: Research Press, 2007.

Willard, Nancy E. *Cyber-Safe Kids, Cyber-Savvy Teens: Helping Young People Learn to Use the Internet Safely and Responsibly*. New York, NY: Jossey-Bass, 2007.

Wolny, Philip. *Foursquare and Other Location-Based Services: Checking In, Staying Safe, and Being Savvy*. New York, NY: Rosen Central, 2012.

BIBLIOGRAPHY

Bartz, Andrea, and Brennan Ehrlich. "To Unfriend or Not to Unfriend: That Is the Facebook Question." CNN.com, September 1, 2010. Retrieved November 2011 (http://articles.cnn.com/2010-09-01/tech/netiquette.unfriending_1_friend-request-facebook-jug-band?_s=PM:TECH).

BullyingStatistics.org. "Cyber Bullying Statistics." 2009. Retrieved November 2011 (http://www.bullyingstatistics.org/content/cyber-bullying-statistics.html).

Fitton, Laura, Michael E. Gruen, and Leslie Poston. *Twitter for Dummies*. Hoboken, NJ: Wiley Publishing, Inc., 2010.

Friend, Elianne. "Woman Fined to Tune of $1.9 Million for Illegal Downloads." CNN.com, June 18, 2009. Retrieved November 2011 (http://articles.cnn.com/2009-06-18/justice/minnesota.music.download.fine_1_jury-instructions-fined-sheryl-crow?_s=PM:CRIME).

Gardner, Susannah, and Shane Birley. *Blogging for Dummies*. Hoboken, NJ: Wiley Publishing, Inc. 2010.

Gosney, John W. *Blogging for Teens*. Boston, MA: Thomson Course Technology PTR, 2004.

Griddle, Linda. *Look Both Ways: Help Protect Your Family on the Internet*. Seattle, WA: Microsoft, 2006.

Griffith, Eric. "Password Protection: How to Create Strong Passwords." PCMag.com, November 29,

2011. Retrieved December 2011 (http://www.
pcmag.com/article2/0,2817,2368484,00.asp).

InternetSafety101.org. "Social Networking Statistics."
2010. Retrieved November 2011 (http://www
.internetsafety101.org/Socialnetworkingstats.htm).

Kallos, Judith. *Email Etiquette Made Easy*. Raleigh, NC:
Lulu.com, 2007.

Kornblum, Janet. "Teens Wear Their Hearts on Their
Blog." *USA Today*, October 30, 2005. Retrieved
November 2011 (http://www.usatoday.com/tech/news/
techinnovations/2005-10-30-teen-blogs_x.htm).

Marklein, Mary Beth. "Survey: Educators Lack Training
to Teach Online Safety." *USA Today*, May 4, 2011.
Retrieved November 2011 (http://www.usatoday
.com/news/education/2011-05-04-online-safety-
students-schools_n.htm).

McFedries, Paul. *Twitter Tips, Tricks, and Tweets.*
Hoboken, NJ: Wiley Publishing, Inc., 2010.

Nelms, Dan. "Social Networking Growth Stats and
Patterns." SocialMediaToday.com, June 16, 2011.
Retrieved November 2011 (http://socialmediatoday
.com/amzini/306252social-networking-growth-stats
-and-patterns).

O'Keeffe, Gwenn Schurgin. *CyberSafe: Protecting and
Empowering Kids in the Digital World of Texting,
Gaming, and Social Media*. Elk Grove Village, IL:
American Academy of Pediatrics, 2011.

Oliver, Dan. *500 Internet Hints, Tips, and Techniques.* Hove, England: Rotovision, 2008.

Reinberg, Steven. "U.S. Kids Using Media Almost 8 Hours a Day." *Bloomberg Businessweek*, January 20, 2010. Retrieved November 2011 (http://www .businessweek.com/lifestyle/content/healthday/ 635134.html).

Sagolla, Dom. *140 Characters: A Style Guide for the Short Form.* Hoboken, NJ: Wiley Publishing, Inc., 2009.

Shipley, David, and Will Schwalbe. *Send: Why People Email So Badly and How to Do It Better.* Rev. ed. New York, NY: Borzoi Books, 2008.

Steele, Jeffrey. *Email: The Manual: Everything You Should Know About Email Etiquette, Policies, and Legal Liability Before You Hit Send.* Portland, OR: Marion Street Press, Inc., 2006.

Strawbridge, Matthew. *Netiquette: Internet Etiquette in the Age of the Blog.* Ely, England: Software Reference, Ltd., 2006.

WarningSigns.com. "Chat Room Dangers." 2010. Retrieved November 2011 (http://www.warningsigns .info/chat_rooms_warning_signs.htm).

Weaver, Jane. "Teens Tune Out TV, Log On Instead." MSNBC, July 24, 2011. Retrieved November 2011 (http://www.msnbc.msn.com/id/3078614/ns/ technology_and_science-tech_and_gadgets/t/teens- tune-out-tv-log-instead/#.TuP1CWPNItM).

ABOUT THE AUTHOR

Tamra Orr is the author of numerous books for readers of all ages. In the course of conducting research for her book projects, she is on the computer almost every waking hour and has learned to take extra precautions to stay safe and virus-free. If she forgets or gets careless, her youngest child comes in and rescues her before the computer melts down. Orr is a graduate of Ball State University and now lives in Oregon with her husband, kids, dog, and cat.

PHOTO CREDITS

Cover © iStockphoto.com/Nikada; p. 5 © Albuquerque Journal/ZUMA Press; p. 10 Comstock/Thinkstock; p. 16 © Richard Sennott/MCT/Landov; p. 19 © ImageForge/Alamy; p. 24 © Eric Nathan/Alamy; p. 30 © ipm/Alamy; pp. 34, 47 © AP Images; p. 37 Jupiterimages/Creatas/Thinkstock; p. 43 Purestock/Thinkstock; p. 51 Justin Sullivan/Getty Images; interior background graphic, back cover phyZick/Shutterstock.com.

Designer: Nicole Russo; Photo Researcher: Amy Feinberg